The Best of

Burnham Book Festival

2023

Introduction

Lewis Coleman

Last year, Burnham Book Festival was all a bit of an experiment. We didn't know whether Burnham-on-Sea wanted this, indeed, whether our sleepy old town was even ready for it. Then we announced the competition and were blown away by the response, over 200 entries from all over Somerset.

This year, we had even more, after opening it up to the whole country. But despite receiving entries from as far afield as Cambridge and County Durham, most of those on the shortlists, which make up our second anthology, are from the South West – creative bunch as we are. 33 authors, with different styles and genres. Some of the writings are funny, some clever, some poignant, and some incredibly powerful.

As a writer myself, it's been a pleasure and a privilege to be a part of this process, as one of the panel sifting through the entries. It took time to arrive at a shortlist we felt content to pass onto the judges – and each of us were sad to see one or two not make the cut. Thank you to all those who entered and a massive congratulations to those who made the shortlists.

A big thanks to our judges, Tara Arkle; Tangent Books publisher, Richard Jones; Diamond Books author and publisher, Jeff Dowson, and author Lu Hersey. And, finally, a huge thank you to all who attended Burnham Book Festival 2023 and purchased a copy of this anthology of superb work. We hope you enjoy them as much we did!.

Poetry

11 & Under Poetry

The World Poem

Freya Jeffries

Leaves grow on trees and bees sting and people get married with a ring.

People dance and Gazelle's prance.

Ninjas that fight wear a belt that's too tight.

People go out for a drink tonight and talk and talk all night.

People pray and there's 24hrs in a day.

Snow falls from the sky and flowers grow and die.

Girls have parties and curls in their hair and dance around with their arms in the air.

Everyone eats and has feet.

Cheetahs run and some people like buns.

People have legs and some people eat eggs.

Fish have gills and people watch films.

Some people give and all people live.

Love is like a dove, it spreads it's wings around these things and this the world poem.

My Special Place on Earth

Charlie Neilson-Pritchard

I love the earth,
One place in particular:
A room
Where I feel comfortable.

When I'm here
I can read in peace,
I can eat in peace
And I can be myself in peace.

I love this place
And everything inside it,
The neon lights that glow,
The cosy, soft bed
And the small basket in the corner.

My favourite part of it
Is a giant teddy
That I can lay on and
Dream big dreams.

I know you won't believe me,
But I'll tell you anyway,

About the jar of pennies at the
Bottom of the basket, that might
Make me a millionaire one day.

This is my special place.

Animals

Ella Bond

From spots to stripes to feathers galore,
And fur and blubber and loads more.
There are birds and beetles and bouncy kangaroos,
And big cats and Polar bears and white cockatoos.
Some animals are nocturnal and stay out at night,
And some have big teeth which give you a fright.
Animals have habitats, they live happily there,
Some go in caves like the brown, grizzly bear.
Some habitats are lost, now a wreck and a mess,
And lots of trees are going down, gradually less and less.
Mankind are destroying our earth's peaceful scene,
The animals try to warn us but we don't know what they mean.
Now some birds are homeless, left sad and distressed,
So where will they now build their twiggy, little nests?
But that's just the start, there's another threat forming,
Some animals have to suffer from Global warming!
For example, the Polar bears up in the North,
The sun comes down, sending them running back and forth.
We need to stand up for the animal's ways,
Even if it takes years, months or days.
So we'll all try our best, give them rights too,
And we all need to help them, including YOU!

Pig

Charlotte Robinson

She is the very ugly pig,

She hates being told

She is pretty and unique

She makes sure to remind herself

"You're so terrible and dull"

No one ever tells her

"You are perfect and beautiful"

She's always been reminded

She's useless and mean

No one ever thinks

She's kind and sweet.

(Read bottom up)

Forest

Hazel Bruce

Rain falls as thunder booms, the breathtaking flowers start to bloom.

Alarming things are happening, we need to help stop them.

Indigenous people follow tracks, some uncontacted, some unfound.

Nightime predators roam around, taking animals to the ground.

Fires take place for farming land it is bad, it is out of hand.

Ocelots, dots all over their body, move swiftly through the trees.

Riots of colour explode all around, bursts of light, bursts of bright.

Exquisite flowers cover the ground, they're amazing you'll see look around.

Swathes of forest come crashing down.

Time is running out to save the forest!

Fear

Bella Thomson

My heart was pounding
My hands were sweaty
Scared

My head was reeling
My legs were shaking
Frightened

My fingers were clasped
My spine shivered
Terrified

I looked down into the vast pit of porcelain
I screamed
The spider ran down the plug hole.

Little Miss Perfect

Janine Cipres

Little miss perfect, Little miss perfect
On time, in line & a prefect.
She's talented, she's liked, her best she always tries
But her self standards just keep getting high.

One wrong move, "It's all over"
As she sobs in the comforting dark, she whispers.
High achiever, she always strives to be
Seems like it's never enough, you see.

Tired and lonely, so anxious and stressed
When she makes a mistake she feels she is less.
But it's okay, it'll be alright
It's all worth it for the success, right?

We always give our all 'cause it feels nice to be the best.
But hey, don't forget it's okay to take a rest

12 to 18 Poetry

This is me

Jacob Hoyes

I`ve been doing this for thousands of years
Meandering here and there
The odd oxbow lake forming,

Humans are here
I hate them!
Always dumping things in me
Every time you flush the toilet
I get your waste

Used to have lots of curves in
But now I`m straight
Thanks to you!

People used to drink from me,
Not any more
I`m disgusting and smelly

I kill wildlife
Every day
That`s the job you gave me

Daily factories
Discharge garbage
Into me

At my mouth
I discharge
my vile waste

Me the Mist

Isobel Saba Grace

Me, a rope of mist circling the castle,
> climbing in circles of unforgiving sorrow.
Me, a cloak of silent, never ceasing unease,
> chains of melancholy suffering.
Me, a wall of impassable regret,
> a pitiful stifling of festivity and amusement.

My work is not done...

I am as silent as the owl on the wing,
> I can cry like the eagle too.
Rushing through the soot stained chimneys,
> I can whistle like the wind in the trees.

My work is not done...

I skim the streets, and the pavements,
> They are my friends, we are cold as ice, we never
> give in.
I whisper my words of wisdom to the stones of Dismal
Drive,
> I do not rest.

My work is not done...

I am free, but when I am near, you are not.
You cannot escape my cage;
        there is no way out.
You cannot break away from my grasp;
        I am stronger than the world.
You cannot cut my chains;
        I am invincible.

My work is not done...

I have a heart of steel.
I am indifferent to your suffering;
        I do not feel.
I see you cry;
        I do not cry too.
I see you in pain;
        I do not feel the pain.
I see you in defeat;
        I have won.

My work is done here…

But, I will return, mark - my - words.

Graduation

Kelly Yu

The dregs of summer choke its remaining greenery
Hydrangeas cry out in their obnoxious glory
Too sheltered, too purple to hold
This is the perfect place:
Heartbreak smeared across the washing line

Linen folding, refolding into itself
It is the cold that kills me
The kindling more weaponry than warmth.
Darkness blinks its fluorescent eyes, its colours arbitrary.
My pupils take in nothing.
I am no less confused than the day I was born.

The gateway to heaven is closer than you think.
This moment through the window
The patio, the child's shoes suspended at the doorway
Here twilight descends an hour too soon
The sun resurfaces only for another cruel dawning

This, this is it? You call this Youth?
Thank you for the epiphanies crushing my windpipe
I have choked up enough flowers to build a garden - is that
    it?
You must be joking, you have to be joking.
There was nothing sweet about my 16.

At the gate, I would rather have known no love, no you

I would've chosen solitude

Just me, and the patio, and my childhood thrashing at the
    doorway

Just me, and the pinkening sky, and glass-light burning
    into my eyelids

The sun drowns in its oceans

Until then, here, now, the dog's bark shaping the evening

Until then.

Wash your dishes. Can't you see? The sky is drowning.

A 'Nice' Painting

Petra Rihan

Someone approaches you; and asks you what you think of
    it
The canvas in front of you
You ponder what to reply.

Mildew
A paintbrush left untouched
By a bowl of strawberry leaves – the fruit long gone
Something romantic about the image left on the easel
It seems so unfair
For something to be so beautiful

Beautiful does not go far enough
No; not for this painting
It is not sufficient
It is like the scent of a lavender leaf
It is like a motif in a story

It is the kind of thing you wish you could bury yourself in
Drown yourself in
Be overtaken by the soft pinks and lilacs and the sage
    greens
An urge to have it be a memory
To dance in it, have your skirt become tangled by grass
For it to make you feel like dancing in rain;

That feeling when you forget about the fact you'll have to
    wash the clothes

And instead enjoy the droplets on your face

Let it take you away to a time

When things were good, like childhood

Not a worry

You yearn to smell the daisies and roses

You desire for the picture to simply wrap you up in a
    blanket of comfortable comfort

Running your calloused fingers over soft acrylic

Brushing over the imperfections that make it so
    incredulous

A sinewy kind of story that it tells

No - that it whispers

Like a secret

You stare for so long

Before you forget

You no longer reminisce over the lavender, over the
    acrylic, over the sinewy secrets

You put away the brushes

Hang it on a wall

It slips away

Like water through fingers

Because yet, you have no way to put this into words

The feelings gripping you in the gut, the tears stinging
  behind your eyes

You think perhaps that it's silly

So instead you reply.

"It's nice."

Be Water, My Friend

Kelly Yu

Be Water, My Friend[1]

and run

until the liquid that runs down your arm no longer scalds

until your voice steams the air,

and the world is not burning

until molten iron cannot be mistaken for gunfire

until you no longer drown in your own oceans

until a song doesn't drive you to tears

until my pen can flow in cursive letters,

and I write my name without shame

until man4 zyu2[2] wrangles her way back into the chinese
dictionary,

and the surface is broken

until a poem written in the dark lives after dawnbreak

until you are no longer Glorious

but merely Free

So run

My Friend

And Be Water

---

[1] Note: A slogan during the Hong Kong protests. Once the police have caught wind of the protestors' location, they will disperse and re-congregate to a new location in order to evade the police. Hence the slogan, 'Be Water'

[2] Definition: Democracy in Cantonese

Changing Tides

Ben Shaw-Young

I walk along
the silent beach, planets
clutched tightly in my grasp.
Beach deserted, no prying eyes
to see me carrying the world they
live on, glowing like fireflies. Waving
at me, the sea glistens under the
full moon, cool sand tickles my feet,
long grass performs ballet in the
light breeze. I sit alone, on the
sand, watching the
sea.

A sudden storm
comes from nowhere. The sea
grows fierce, waves monstrously tall
as mountains.   Confusion.   Terror.
The Earth   in my hand   cracks,
starts to   break   aw a y .
Looking around all I can
see is destruct i o n.
Sand turns grey.
Grass burns.

Something is wrong.

The Earth begins to slip from my hand.

Turning it round I see a giant sinkhole,

swallowing the planet, eating it alive.

Furiously, I try to fill it in.

It doesn't work.

All I can do is watch helplessly as the Earth is

de s t r o y e   d.

In the Unlikely Event

Kelly Yu

Of rain
I am flooded in the basement
I scream, flail my arms a bit
And you crash through the door
I will weep into your arms like you know me

Snapstring, a twang, a mouthful of blood
We simply do not die the same
And only my hand remains unlovable

Fine, you can have your bathetic silences, and
while I fall
I will carry with me the weight of a crescendo
The burst that burned too bright

And I'm sorry your first love did not end in rain
I loved you too much and forgot to make it beautiful

In the unlikely event I needed saving
I will let you kiss my brow
In the distance, my dreams heave their final sigh
The light has flooded in
The basement remains a basement

19+ (Adult) Poetry

Ark (what would you take?)

Jan Martin

I'd like to take the best of me:
my heart, the bit that's left
my soul, the bit that's good
my mind, the bits that work,

and leave behind the rest:
the way I sometimes
see devils
and hallucinate dirty electricity,
my tendency to think in spirals.

But when the flood comes cresting in
and I reach for heart and soul
against an implacable wave,
they sink like sponges
and leave me
clutching at debris
under monumental seas.

That's when fear
pulls me up,
anger delivers me,
and sadness
becomes a raft.

Ark is
the devil that brings you home.

Sweet Memory Sounds

Ben Banyard

i.m. Derek "DJ Derek" Serpell-Morris (1941-2015)

The sunlight's blue in cigarette smoke.
He sits on a stool at the bar, nodding his head
to another record from his collection,
the blackest white man in Bristol
who was lifted up by the first generation
of Jamaicans to come here.

When his marriage imploded
and he packed in his job at Fry's,
this bespectacled accountant,
always suited, smart, respectable,
found a basement flat in St Pauls
in which to stash his breakdown.

It was lucky, then, that he knew
The Star & Garter on a corner in Montpelier,
where the regulars slapped down dominoes,
cackled into their Guinness,
demanded only the finest music
to remind them of home.

Men and women of his own age
from an era riveted by the Empire,
they have more in common than you'd think,

take him as one of their own in this city
with so much blood on its hands.

Selecting tunes for them is a community service.
Mi feel mi back-a-yard!
they say, as the tunes spin
and his patois comes naturally,
no insult: it happens as the reggae seeps in.

And from here he travels up and down,
carts his gaffer-taped record boxes
on buses and trains to towns and cities
that need to hear him play,
whether they know it or not.

Driving

Nyika Suttie

Hoar frost whitens the trees
Pheasants block my way to work
And the other day you nearly
Crashed out of this world.
I haven't processed it yet.
I drove to find you,
Bruised, pride wounded.
I'd cross deserts for you, darling,
Even drive through Birmingham.
"Cars are replaceable, you are not"
I said.
It occurs to me as I drive
That you are more irreplaceable than
The icicles, the pink sky
The pheasants, and the Mendips
And the rare, precious, hoar frost.

Taxidermist
Macaque

Obsidian eyes unblink the rink
Of ceiling, brink of man, boiled
Bones with glue for sinew, and
Soft dry skin. The man tweezers in
The cotton flesh, probing, tearing, palpating
To extremities. An effort of

Devotion, he stuffs it with
His loneliness. Shell of man, he fills
This husk of beast with self, his own
Wants and hurts and passions, his
Honeycomb heart, stretches tenderly,
Stiches delicately, feels the affinity,

Four glassy eyes polished bright.

My Lexicon Lover

Mandy Woods

Your grammar is perfect, your syntax divine,
Your years so well spent learning how to decline,
Your apostrophe usage, it's always sublime,
Irrefutably beautiful, won't you be mine?

Your Scrabble vocabulary knocks me dead,
Multisyllabic from A through to Z,
So attractive I find you, it has to be said,
The word 'pulchritudinous' won't leave my head!

Your IQ's sky high, and I find that it tends
To inspire all manner of things in my head,
A haiku, a ballad, a song without end,
My lexico-sexagenarian friend!

Double entendres and off-colour puns
Suggestively, recklessly trip off my tongue;
The future looks perfect if you'll just become
My voluptuous, sumptuous one.

I know it's intense, but I once had a dream
Where together we'd leafed through a whole diction'ry,
You'd seemed like the pluperfect partner for me,
My lexicon lover, my queen spelling bee!

A Hunger to be Heard

Jan Martin

A crow sets down on the path today
good-bad-luck message bird,
with her bright black eye and nodding head
a book, that struggles to be read
and hungers to be heard.

The gulls like bright white fireworks
fall fading in between
the crest and crash of their wild short lives,
in swooping lifts and crushing dives,
they're screaming to be seen.

My bright boy from his hideaway
plays his dreams to me,
a head of songs and heart of hope,
from the other end of a telescope
he sings for us to see.

Wailing child and whining dog
bully, bore and seer
shout in defiance of deadening lull
we begin with the word, and word is all
and we exist to hear

We are huge in our insignificance,
bigger than the whole wide world,
calling out as we're curling down
to the place where sea-stopped sailors drown,
singing songs to the wide star crown,
and hungry to be heard.

#90 Dream

Richard Leslie

Whassup? Morning glory in my childhood single bed.

I'm dreaming, then the sun comes up, and Princess Di is
dead.

Jenny kissed me when we met, I order my first beer.

The generation two above are all still here.

The love of my life's dumped me, but I only just met her.

So don't look back in anger, things can only get better.

School is out forever and at last I'm free.

Those who feel the breath of sadness, sit down next to me.

Friends is on the tele, and Three Lions is getting sung.

Gazza over Hendry's head, and I am still young.

One of them is Ginger, one is Scary, one is Scouse.

We all know if we roll with it, we'll get our country house.

May day! May day! A new dawn has broken, has it not?

I'm buzzin' with the Cellnet mobile phone that I've just got.

I know you're cooking dinner, Mum, but I'm out with my
friend you see.

She's got one in the oven, but it's nothing to do with me.

United win the treble, we're the class of '99.

We all put on our sunscreen and go giggling back to mine.

A brimful of asha's on my Grandpa's 45s.

The towers are still standing. We're all still alive.

I know I'll pass the test soon. I just need to stop the stalling.
Still dreaming, then I'm rudely awakened by the dustman
     calling.
Grass and sun, a beautiful morning, wake up, Boo!
There really are so very many things for us to do.

Somehow I closed my eyes though. It was only for a second.
All the lights that led the way were there for us, I reckoned.
But the fountain down the road now seems so very far away.
Was it not us and all our friends there just the other day?

When we woke up that morning we had no way of knowing
That we wouldn't even notice all the years coming and going.
Slow down. Hold on! Where's everyone I knew then gone?
In love, in fear, in hate, in tears, hold on. Hold on.

The Unsayable Absence: Selina

Anstice Fisher

that last outing we walked round the lake
    slow
        halting
            your lungs weak now

    you laughed as the great crested grebes
dived and bobbed

        like teapots upside down you said

water rippled from purple to green
    red to cobalt
        birds plants clouds

    broken up and undulating
as if we walked round your life

    dipped refracted
breaking through surface to depth
        the pattern and meaning protean

and saw how water and tears
    like bodies
    like life
        become liquefaction

like writing with water
    becomes transparent
        dissolves

for a moment your kabuki face
floats white in the lake of my eye.

Poet's Retreat

Macaque

Here at midday the shadows
Of the apple trees are veins of infinite black.
The whole yard is still as marble.

From the edge of the heat waders warble
Out of sight, their throats slack
Like the wisteria hanging in rows

Along the south wall. The smell of bladder wrack
And the salty sound of a thousand pebbles
Jostling under the rhythmic throes

Of the turning tide impose
Upon this still and silent haven the burble
Of the outside world, everything I want the knack

Of forgetting – the tick of the clock I didn't unpack,
Memento mori of the endless jumble
Of commuting, commerce, chaos. I just want to repose,

Enjoy the garden, compose not decompose,
Wait in the shade for an apple to tumble,
Delight in the scent of cinnamon as it cracks.

Short Stories

11 & Under Short Stories

Space Lamb
Ellie Smith

On a misty winter morning, a little lamb called Frieda was born. She was born in a modern sort of shed, a so-called barn.

A few hours later, a strange shiny plate came flying overhead. Large beams of light started to flood the field. Though Frieda was only born mere hours ago, she was smart, a very smart sort of smart. She was a miniscule little thing with knobbly knees and fleece as soft as a cloud.

Being inquisitive, she wandered outside to get a closer look at the beams of light.

"AH-HA!" it burst into her brain like a popping piece of popcorn. "It's a UFO!".

Frieda saw the other sheep running around panicking. Her instinct was to do the right thing. As she tried to reassure the others something horrifying happened! Frieda could see the UFO's trapdoor opening.

A beam of light shone down and up flew Bella, who was Frieda's Mum. She couldn't believe it! Her Mum, gone, vanished!

Frieda couldn't let her emotions get the better of her. Her brain whizzed into action as she thought of a plan.

Frieda would build a rocket to follow her Mum into space. She set right to it, building all day and night hoping that Bella would be alright. Frieda built the rocket from things around the farm and it looked a bit higgly-piggly. After a few test runs and tweaks, the ride was up and running (by this point it looked a lot better) Finally, all done!

Frieda also crafted an astronaut's helmet; she put it on, sat in her straw seat and clipped herself in.

3, 2, 1….BLAST OFF!

The little lamb zoomed through space, amazed by the view. Seeing millions of stars blew her mind. It was incredible!

Five minutes later a massive asteroid came crashing down onto Frieda's rocket. Sending her off course as a hurl of jumbled confusion came buzzing through her head as everything went black…

As she woke, Frieda realised she wasn't in her rocket or in the barn. Where could she be?

Frieda could just make out the tall silver bars. It hit her…she was in a prison!?! She was now wide awake, her head still hurting from the crash. She jumped to her feet, everything still blurry. Frieda tried to walk but she still felt wobbly. As her vision cleared she saw another sheep asleep in the cell, unbelievably, it was her Mum.

"Mum?" she shouted.

"Frieda!!" came a groggy reply. "I can't believe it's you. You found me!"

"We need to find a way out of this musty, dusty place!" exclaimed Frieda.

Seeing the window was open, they climbed up and escaped into the rocket park (like a car park but for UFOs).

They spotted a rocket with an open door, snuck in and slammed the hatch shut. The tricky two ran to the control panel, found the start button and blasted off. They looked at each other and smiled knowing they were safely heading home.

The Coming of the Spuds

Lowen Delbridge

It was a dull, dark day in the planet of Spudnado and the Spuds were looking for a planet to stay on when they saw planet Earth.

The Spuds decided "This is a very good planet, with water and food to feed us forever".

So the Spuds decided to invade this mysterious planet. So the Spuds planned their attack on this planet. Their plan was to hide in a cave and do a surprise attack.

The Spuds got in their Spudmobiles and got all geared up.

They put their armour on and got in their vehicles.

The Spud's armour was:

- A steel helmet with a glass visor
- A carrot gold plate with iron spikes on the back
- Red leather boots with knots
- White, hard marble gloves with silver spikes on the end
- Leg and arm guards with golden, iron and steel ingots.

They were ready to invade Earth! Spudnado was the first planet to try and invade Earth; everyone knew that Earth had the best armour, weapons and resources but that was all going to change today.

Earth's armour was:

- Emerald helmet
- Iron plate
- Silver gloves
- Marble boots

- Most importantly diamond guards for legs and arms.

Their weapons were all made of wood and Iron:

- Swords
- Shields
- Bow, arrow and crossbow.

So the Spuds got into the Spudmobiles and flew up, up and away into the dark, night sky.

As stars glittered all around them, they could already hear the chanting in their heads, 'Spud! Spud! Spud!' they all dreamed off to sleep in their little tiny saucers just the size for a potato.

When they all woke up they saw green grass and blue sky; it was the most wonderful thing these Spuds had ever seen in their little Spud lives.

It was brilliant, way better than their horrific planet; it was warm and full of hiding places to hide from the people. They found a good cave to hide in whilst they thought up a fantastic plan.

Their plan was to hide for a few days or weeks until they where all geared up and ready to go. Then, on the surprise attack, pounce up on the people and declare Earth a conquered planet.

No longer a safe peaceful planet but a planet filled with utter chaos and destruction. Their plan was definitely foolproof and would not fail like all of their other plans before.

To be continued…..

The Alchemist

Adam Egan

Many moons ago, in a small village at the edge of a forest, lived a family. Nicholas, the father, was an alchemist. The mother, Mary, was a beautiful sweetheart with hair as dark as a raven. But the true joy and love of this family was an eight-year-old boy called Veridean. He was tall, handsome with a clean mop of dark hair. His smile was like the sun shining down on them both. However, his father was troubled. They were poor and lived a simple life. All Nicholas wanted was the best for his family; he was worried that Veridean might think him a bad father. Something had to change.

Veridean liked nothing more than exploring. One sunny day, he was scampering through the gnarled trees in Hunters Wood when he came across an ancient looking hut. Peering through the window, he couldn't believe his eyes when he saw his father bending over a machine.

The next day, the boy came back to the hut and asked, "Father what are you making?". He explained that this machine could turn ordinary metals into pure, the very purest, gold. After that, his father brought home lavish presents and bagfuls of money. Soon they became the richest family in the village. But, despite all this wealth something strange was happening to Nicholas. He was changing. Instead of exchanging loving words with his family, he scowled and became unbearably sarcastic.

Little did his family know that Nicholas was using his own most treasured memories to power his extraordinary machine. So now when Veridean was in bed he had to listen to his parents' raised voices, sometimes screams. As this carried on Mary visibly aged beyond her years. Her body became as frail and floppy as a rag doll. Eventually she died of sadness and her son didn't even recognise the woman who lay dead before him. His heart torn apart with grief, Veridean ran away.

22 years later...

Veridean, now tall and even more handsome, returned to his childhood home, sure that his father must be dead. Walking through the forest he happened upon his father's old hut. His eyes filled with tears, and he flung open the rickety door. Then he saw it, resting against the huge machine: a tear-stained letter addressed to him. As he picked up the letter, the machine whirred into life. Lights shimmered, glass orbs filled with a cloudy smoke and electricity crackled through the machine. After a few minutes some liquid flowed into a tear-shaped cupula. A drop of the liquid dripped slowly onto a pile of dull grey coins. At once, there was a blinding flash! The coins were pure gold. Enraged, Veridean was determined to have revenge on the machine that had destroyed his father's mind. He decided there and then to end this nightmare and he smashed the machine into tiny fragments. Veridean walked out of that unhappy place never to return, vowing that his life would be forever true and kind.

The Pizza Lion

Leo Wynn

Once upon a time there was a buff, rich man called Bob, he was going on holiday to Italy in his massive, fancy private jet and so he made a delicious, flamboyant pizza lion for the huge, bumpy journey.

Later on, he was ordering his miserable, yet well payed workers, to pack his bags. A few hours later after the bags were packed, in the dead of the night, the pizza lion seemed to vibrate. Bob thought it was just a tiny earth quake, as they happened all the time where he lived, he was used to them, so he rolled over and went back to sleep.

The next day he was flying to Italy in his massive, fancy jet. They were high in the sky, the wind was gusty and powerful. The large, ornate suitcase vibrated in a roar and the delicious, flamboyant pizza lion burst forth and flew out the window!

"Stop please I need you!'' cried Bob

"Fly, fly keep on tryin', you cant catch me, I'm the pizza lion!!'' roared the Pizza Lion. In a instant he flew into a enormous bald eagle with a thump!

Barry the bald eagle was outraged and immediately commenced to try to gobble the pizza lion up!

He went "uumm" cheesy, as he took a nibble from the pizza lions tail.

"Ouch" screamed the pizza lion

"I need to eat you up!" screeched the bald eagle.

The pizza lion pushed Barry away and began to fly

away.

He gave him a silly parting wave, whilst singing.

"Fly, Fly, keep on tryin', you can't catch me I'm the pizza lion!"

All was calm for a time, until there was a mighty crash. The pizza lion had flew straight into a crazy hungry pigeon, who was wolfing down a bag of stolen chips.

The bag exploded and chips went everywhere!

Through the cloud of flying chips, the pigeon saw the pizza lion and said "I need to eat you, please!"

The pizza Lion darted away and replied "Fly, Fly, keep on tryin', you can't catch me I'm the pizza lion"

The pizza lion flew into a invincible, speedy cloud monster! It easily cut off one of the pizza lion's ear and a lot of tomato sauce came out of the pizza lion but the he had to stay focused, the cloud monster tried to hit the pizza lion to cut off his other ear but the tasty hero powered up to 10% and dodged with ease then, astoundingly, the pizza lion's whole ear regenerated. The pizza lion eagerly gave the cloud monster millions of punches then flew down to the ground.

Tales spread across the land about the powerful mighty Pizza Lion who even the cloud monster didn't want to mess with. Every monster, human and creature heard the stories.

The pizza Lion relaxed for the rest of his life and was never bothered again because of his power.

The End

Castle of Wonders

Rebecca Turner

I live in a castle with a thousand corridors. Each corridor leads to a thousand rooms. Each room has a thousand doors. And behind each door are ten million wonders. Every day there would be something new to discover, a new door to open. One morning I might step into a land where gravity does not exist, and I could float free as a cloud as long as I liked. That same afternoon, I might descend into a cave made of darkness, filled with broken mirrors. This was my life, and I loved it.

One morning, seemingly a normal one, I rose from my bed and began imagining what I would find that day. It was a habit of mine - try to guess what would be behind the door. After a hurried breakfast (I lived alone) I chose a corridor at random, walked through into the six hundred and ninety-first room, and opened the sixteenth door. There was only darkness behind it, but I stepped forwards confident I could return.

I emerged into bright sunlight. The door stood behind me, seemingly just a door on its own, although I knew better. I was in a field, with a small house at the end of it. I always found myself unsure what was really behind the doors - were these worlds real, or an illusion? Would the people here remember me? But I didn't really care. As long as I could keep on stepping into a new wonder, I would be happy.

I sat for a few hours in the field, before deciding to return. I reached for the door handle, but it would not turn. I pushed harder. Nothing. That frightened me - what if I couldn't get back? This had never happened before. Suddenly a voice spoke behind me. "Hello? What are you doing here?" I turned, and saw a young girl standing behind me. I was unsure of what to say - tell the truth, or lie? Truth won.

"I'm possibly from a different dimension, trying to get back through this door to my castle of uncountable wonders."

This seemed to surprise her, as though multi-dimensional travellers were a rare occurrence. She thought. Then...

"Have you got a key?" she asked. "Keys open doors." A key! Why hadn't I thought of that? But...

"I don't have a key," I said. She smiled.

"It's your lucky day then. I do." From her pocket, she produced a large silver key. "I found it ages ago. Try it."

I waved the key at the door. Miraculously, impossibly, a keyhole appeared. I slotted the key into the lock, and turned it. The door opened - behind it, I could see my castle.

"Thanks," I said, stepping through. "I might come back sometime." She nodded.

"Sure. Just remember the key!"

I still live in the castle with a thousand corridors. Each corridor leads to a thousand rooms. Each room has a thousand doors. And behind each door are ten million wonders.

The Ground Floor

Ayla Mottram

Suspect Criminal: ????????

Place: Apartment 7, Gale Street, Ground Floor, 2002.

<u>Tuesday</u>

The Secret Detective Society hired me to keep things on track. That is not what I'm doing. It has come to their attention that some children are smarter than you'd expect. Not exactly smart enough to solve mysteries, (any cool child's dream) but to type… words. I was hired to do that. But I found it boring. So, I started investigating myself. In, well, secret.

I go by the name: The Red Falcon, but you can call me Holly.

It's odd, I seem to be a lot better than the SDS's star investigators: Yaxley Normand, the best in the team; Mandy Noraxely, the smartest and John Taylor, the fighter. Being me, I leave specific clues for them to find, so they can try to figure out the crime, but there is a lot of competition between them and they're starting to get quite cut-throat about it. At least they'll never guess it's me helping them…

<u>Thursday</u>

The phone rang in the office.

An ear splitting shriek that ran through the entire building causing the phone to shudder uncontrollably as I picked it up.

"Hello," I said in a gruff, fake accent that disguised my identity.

"There's been a murder! Please, help!" A voice shrieked again, displaying high levels of panic as they breathed in and out heavily.

"Could you tell me where this happened," I asked.

"Apartment 7, Ground Floor, Gale Street! Please, come quick!"

I sped out of the office door.

When I got to the place, I ran inside to find John Taylor dead on the floor with a bloody knife next to him. The knife had an engraving saying: Dora Lynne Maxy. There was a small, purple bag and a spray painted word saying LOVEABLE. Ten people stood gathered around, most looked shocked, but one was still hysterical- the one who I guess had called. According to them, they had all been at a golf club when they came in and found John on the floor. The first thing I thought was about the odd engraving on the knife. Surely it had to mean something. And why the bag and the word? As my brain whirled around with thoughts, I picked up the bag. There were the letters MN on a mirror, but nothing else.

It clicked. MN were initials! But who could they belong to...

Was it Mandy Noraxley? But, yes that would make sense! The name Mandy means loveable and if you rearrange the letters on the knife, that spells Mandy Noraxley!!!

My brain fizzed with excitement, that was so easy! Hmm, suspiciously easy...

Mandy Noraxley is known for her courage and

cleverness. I doubted that she would be so stupid as to leave such obvious clues. Was she being framed? "If you rearrange Dora Lynne Maxy to something else then you get…"

"Yaxley Normand," said a cold voice behind me…

12 to 18 Short Stories

The Hunt

Amelie Hood

Focus. Aim. Shoot.

Arthur fired the shotgun and the pheasant flittered to the ground, a gruesome end to its final flight. Its body littered the ground, joining the many already shot down. He blew the smoke away and reached for the next shell; after 22 years of being taken out on hunting trips with his father, being taught to pursue his prey in a careful, meticulous manner, this action had become a habit. It had become so autonomous, it filled his dreams, and his nightmares too. He could do it blind. Over the years, it had been necessary for him to become desensitised to the bloody corpses left behind, the harrowing squawking of a pheasant or the final scream of a deer as the bullet pierces its skin. Those sounds haven't echoed in his nightmares until he woke up sweating and gasping for air since he was a child, yet it still amazed him how little regard his father had for these innocent souls. He viewed the fowl, hares, and elk purely as 'game'. A sport to be won and mounted over the fireplace with pride. The whole thing was revolting to Arthur.

Animals gravitated naturally to Arthur, as he did to them. Maybe that's why he was such a good shot. They trusted him blindly and he crushed it with a bullet. With every trigger pulled, and every animal blown to pieces, Arthur cringed and desperately tried to retract from the present.

He was just five when he fell in love with nature, and ever since then, the everlasting fall had deepened his admiration for the intricate relationship between flora and fauna. He would spend hours wandering through the woods, fondling the long grass, staring in awe at the dormice and the vultures. He didn't see how any human company could ever compare to the quiet peace that only comes in the dawn of winter mornings over the moors; watching the sun rise as birds twitter and owls hoot and the air is still crisp enough to form a cloud as he breathes. That love, or friendship, or whatever the complicated relationship could be called may have seemed one-sided from an outsider's perspective, yet Arthur knew nature cared for him as much as he did for it. He felt it in the warm caress of a summer breeze, in the gentle tread of a mouse as it scurried along his shoes, in the way he never felt lonely when surrounded by the verdant beauty.

On this particular hunt, he lined up the muzzle, aiming for the deer's shoulder- a quick and, mostly, painless death. The habitual reluctancy overwhelmed Arthur, yet he fought it back- there was no time to dwell when he promised his father he'd impress. He had planned this trip as a guise to show off Arthur's natural aptitude for hunting; those hunts were the only time he felt his father's pride shine fondly onto him, instead of the glaring disappointment that usually came when every year passed, and Arthur remained unmarried and without an heir. The group watched like a hawk, attempting to pick out any flaw or mistake made by Arthur, determined not to be bested by him, however, it was all in vain. Arthur was clearly the finest huntsman around, and the older gentlemen loathed the idea of a renowned failure in society being superior in anything. After all, this boy had always been reserved and unwilling to partake in any social club or governmental ploy. Why is it he had been gifted with this remarkable talent, and not the more esteemed men? Arthur was well aware of the disapproval that followed him around like a plague, and he would not wish it any other way. Whilst many people saw this talent as a gift, he only viewed it as a curse. It may have been the only way he slept at night: with the knowledge that he was not getting away with this crime against nature so easily. His only way into society or winning the favour of his father was to end the lives of such beautiful creatures – creatures that might have starving children waiting for their parent to bring back their next meal. It hurt his heart to think about it, but he forced himself to, in the fear of himself becoming just like his father and his so-called friends if he forgot his morals.

One after one, the shotgun was fired and it became clear that Arthur would not be beaten, so the party resigned and headed off to their respectful homes, each with a prize in tow. This time, Arthur stayed behind. He sat down on a moss-covered log, put his head on his hands, and finally allowed himself to rest. It had been a long day, and he was emotionally and physically exhausted. The regret ate up inside of him, as it always did, yet he didn't allow himself to be consumed by it. He knew that tomorrow, another hunting party would turn up and he would be expected to fell more innocents.

And so, the cycle continued.

Second Hand Magic

Grace Poole

Musty air clogs the space, and dust hangs everywhere, suspended in the little streams of hot golden sunlight that pour in, burrowing their way past the shutters that block most of the late summer glow. Rack of clothes at waist height stretch to the dimly lit, poster-cluttered back wall of the shop, like a maze of dusty garments. The faint mumble of the slow stream of traffic outside drifts in and competes lazily with the drawl of a radio hidden somewhere in the depths. This is a tiny labyrinth of second-hand magic, where turtlenecks and sarong skirts rub shoulders with the stacks of band t-shirts spilling onto the floor in a waterfall of Beatles and ACDC. The whole place has a kind of dreamy aspect, as if reality is thin here and time thick. Seconds and minutes flow oddly. It smells old. Not bad old- but the sweet, dusty, honey scent of forgotten things. Of other people's history and stories folded in unwanted clothing. Endings and beginnings intertwine in places like this. I yank out clothes at random, dust dancing in the sunlit air with every move I make. A biker jacket. A miniskirt. Billowing drawers clearly donated by some Victorian grandmother. I should get going, but I just want to bask in this light-drenched haven for a little longer, hidden from the grasping claws of time.

"Can I help you with anything?"

I almost jump as the figure tucked behind the counter speaks. She's been watching me for a while, as I fill my arms with second-hand spoils. A halo of grey hair and a face full of lines traced by laughter. She's nested in her burrow amid the hangers, the wooden counter with almost drowning under a pile of clothes not yet stickered with price tags. Nestled in a cocoon of trench coats and woolly hats and clothing too time-worn to be sold. It seems, in the dim shadows of the back of the shop, as if she's some kind of mythic creature. It's been so long since she left this place, she's become one with it. The trench coats on their hangers above her become wings while the jerseys and jumpers heaped on her lap are a raggedy wool-knotted tail. Spectacles resting on her forehead are horns that curve from her brow. It should be terrifying, seeing her looming out of the darkness- eldritch, ancient, unknowable- but it's not. This creature, sworn to protect this place. Then the light shifts and it's gone; just an old woman hidden away in her shop.

She smiles gently at me; my heart aches just a little because in that fleeting second, she looks just like my grandma. The pain of missing someone doesn't every really go away but ebbs and flows like the tide, and in that moment I long to see her one more time.

"I'm alright," My voice sounds strange, distorted by the way time folds in on itself in this little cluttered shop. I should go, but the sun paints my back and the song of the stories hidden in this place calls for me. Each and every one of these clothes was held and worn and owned by someone before. I gather my bundle of clothes closer to my chest and make my way to the counter. I don't want to dump them down in case the neat piles serve some purpose, so I just stand clutching them. The woman meets my gaze, tight curls twining close to her head.

"That'll be all?"

"Yes."

She reaches out to take the clothes I hand her.

"You're in here a lot."

Light settles on my skin as she turns on a desk lamp to

see the price tags. The is metal twisted and almost clawing the tiny bulb. Wires trail to the floor and disappear behind her like snakes, seeking a socket. I don't know what to say to that.

"Yes."

Such a conversationalist. I've seen this woman almost every week since I came here and said barely more than a few words, letting my imagination fill in the blanks. Today she's an unearthly creature tucked away from time: next week I'm sure my mind will come up with another space for her to fill. It's fun to dream up lives for other people and the old magic woven into this place just makes it easier.

The truth is, I'm in here because the feeling of this shop calls to me. I miss magic- the type that comes flicking through beaten pages of old books with cracked spines or being surrounded by old and pre-worn clothes. This city is so big, and without the light and warmth from cluttered little shops in winding streets, the hole home left is bigger than ever. It feels like I'm the only person here who ever visits second-hand shops.

Handing over crumpled notes. Offering a smile and bidding her farewell. Every move now feels like stalling. Light cascades over my skin, and the smell of dust has never been so inviting, and I don't want to leave. But it's late- the sun will slip behind the skyline soon and I have to get home. I smile at her as I go. This city is so big and it's nice to have a crowded messy little refuge in this corner.

The old woman rises from her chair and her age-lined face is lit with a gentle warmth. Coats and scarves fall from around her as her wings rise, almost touching the ceiling with their leathery tips. Shrouds of magic slip away as she lets go of the illusion. Streaks of light brush her horns. Perceptive, that one was. Almost saw through. She navigates crammed boxes and tilting stacks to peek between the blinds and catch a last glimpse of the figure darting between cars into the distance. Another who feels it, her mind seems to whisper. Another who knows the pull of the magic woven between the threads of cast-offs. Second-hand magic.

Consequences

Alex Shaw-Young

Memories pour through my mind as I stand staring at the silently-grieving figures, crumbling and bent like ancient tombstones, under the relentless drizzle outside the church. Not for the first time this week I wonder whether things could have been different if I had only been brave enough. Unbidden, my thoughts take me to that moment only weeks ago.

Books fell to the floor, bruised spines silently protesting as they lay in painfully contorted positions amongst the half-finished homework and half empty pens. The boy sat in the centre of the chaos, his tormentors looming like mountains above him.

"Come on, we're going to miss the bell," my friends urged. I felt so helpless and torn. I paused briefly before I continued to walk.

Away.

Away from the boy who so obviously needed a friend.

Away from the broken books and their broken spines.

Feigning ignorance. A puppet of society. Just like everyone else. I didn't see the pleading sorrowful eyes alone and downcast, nor did I hear the barely audible remark made by a friend or at least I chose not to, it wasn't my problem I thought it wasn't like he was my friend. I felt sympathy for him, yes, but it wasn't my place to interfere. I stood by and did nothing.

I was wrong. I should have tried to be a friendly face. They found him, his parents. Hanging limp and lifeless the next day. The news shot through the school like wild-fire suffocating the air from everyone's lungs.

Regret flows through my veins like ice, as I watch the coffin's final journey borne stoically on shrunken shoulders and I know this feeling will never leave me, not until I lie on my own deathbed. He will never grow up, never marry, never have children and grandchildren. His future, once a blank slate now just a cold grave marked Austin Rivers. Guilt envelops me; I watch Austin's mum enter the church, head bowed, stifling sobs as she clutches the tiny hand of his sister. The vicar moves to greet them and then, in that brief moment time seems to freeze and I catch a glimpse of another world where things turned out differently, where I was brave enough.

Memories pour through my mind as I step slowly into the sunlit church, guiding me to that moment so long ago.

Books fell to the floor, bruised spines silently protesting as they lay in painfully contorted positions amongst the half-finished homework and half empty pens. The boy sprawled in the centre of the chaos helpless against the brutish tormentors looming above him.

"Come on, we're going to miss the bell," my friends urged. I felt so torn and helpless as I watched them humiliate him. I turned to leave, but then his eyes caught mine and within them I saw all the pain and sorrow he was desperately trying to hold back. I looked over my shoulder, not a teacher in sight. Just the hustle of the many students shouldering their way through the crowded corridor feigning ignorance, muffling their sniggers behind closed palms and closed minds at the scene before them. It was at that moment that all my anger flared up. Why did nobody seem to care? Why was nobody intervening? Why wasn't I?

I was about to turn away when I heard one of my

friends mutter, "What does it matter? He has no friends anyway."

I paused briefly.

Without a word, I walked purposefully towards him, ignoring the shocked gasps of my 'friends' behind me, the malicious tormentors already summoned by the bells of hell. I hand him his books, creased pages and bent spines still fixable. He offered me a weak smile and then after every pen, book and paper was stowed safely in his bag we passed our separate ways.

"Hi," I said cautiously. "Do you mind if I sit here?"

He looked up at me, his eyes surprised. He nodded suspiciously, worried it was another trick sent to antagonise him. I sat with him at lunch that day and many days afterwards. His name was Austin, Austin Rivers. We became good friends. There were times when he would be quiet almost as if he were lost deep within himself, trapped in some dark corner of his mind. Over time though, he crept out of his shell. I helped him to stand against his demons and he helped me to face mine as well. Later, I would tell him how although over the years I had lost my friends I had gained the only one that mattered.

Years went by and we went from friends, to lovers, to our wedding.

I pause at the end of the aisle and take a deep breath; drinking him in, staring into his sea blue eyes, once so full of sorrow now reflecting joy and happiness throughout the church and I smile. Austin smiles back at me and for a second we are the only two people in the world. The vicar begins the ceremony, yet time seems to stand still, and for a brief, horrifying moment I catch a tiny glimpse of a world where I wasn't brave enough.

A Rescue Cat's Journey

Arabella Turner

I lay curled in my nest, Mother Cat standing above me. One full moon had passed since I had come into the world, and I was starting to find my paws. My littermates were lying next to me, mewling and crying for food. Mother Cat touched each one with her nose, reassuring us that all was well.

I watched as Mother Cat picked up Older Brother in her mouth. She trotted out of the nest, carrying him tenderly. She took each one in turn out and away. It wasn't long before I was left alone. She promised she'd come back, told me to wait, and then strode off. It was the last time I'd ever see Mother Cat.

Nobody was around. Carefully, I climbed out of the pile of cardboard, and up onto a low wall nearby. Why should I stay put? The cold night air wrapped around me, pulling at my fur. I began to waddle forwards, my shaking legs carrying me over to the towering house nearby. I climbed steadily, first onto the bins, then onto the garage, then the gutter. I was high up now, and the ground swayed below me. Looking up all I could see was the starless darkness of night.

The wind began to pick up. Now I was scared. Where was Mother Cat? I cried out, but my tiny voice was drowned out by the howling wind. Rain began to fall, spitting at my fur. I was hungry and cold. I tried to get down, but I couldn't retrace my steps. I was too weak and tired.

Days passed, and Mother Cat didn't come. The Wind Monster tried to pull me off the roof. It made me wet, and cold, and scared. It made me so hungry I couldn't think. It took Mother Cat from me. Time seemed to flow slowly. Soon, I knew, I would start the Long Sleep everyone feared; the one that wouldn't end.

When all hope had left me and I was lying helpless on the roof, someone must have seen me. I found myself lifted off and taken down, not by Mother Cat but by a human. I was too weak to protest. It talked to some others of its kind for a while, before shutting me in a dark box. Scared cat scent filled my nose. I tried to cry, but no sound came out.

They took me somewhere foul-smelling and poked me and looked in my eyes and mouth. What could I do? They were much stronger than I was, and I had no idea how to get out. I lay there, letting them do what they wanted. It didn't matter to me anymore.

Eventually I was sent off with one of the humans. I got to go inside one of the houses that I once sheltered beside. It smelt of other cats, but I couldn't see any. The human here was a very strange individual. It produced milk out of an item in its hands, and made me suck it every few hours.

After some days I was carted off to another place. I was shut in a Cage, surrounded by other terrified cats. They fed me and played with me, but it was impersonal. There was no space to run around, and no fresh air. At night I would cry for Mother Cat to come back, knowing all the time that she couldn't.

Then there was the growling machine. I had been forced inside it by some humans I'd never seen, shut in a box, when it started to roar. It got right to my bones. I was being bounced around, using all my energy trying not to be sick. It was such a horrible, unnatural feeling.

At long last I was let out of the box. I found myself in a huge room, the humans standing around me. They spoke in soft voices and moved slowly. The lowest layer of the cat tree seemed like a huge way up, and I couldn't reach my litter tray at all. At two moons, I was much smaller than the cat it was designed for. Still, it was a warm, welcoming place.

That night I barely slept. What would happen to me next? This place seemed alien to me, but it was nice nonetheless. Would I have to go back to the Cage? Or, even worse, back to the roof where the Wind Monster lurked. I began to panic, and ran behind a propped up row of boards against a wall.

When one of the humans came down in the morning, it took a long time for them to find me. When I was finally discovered, I was furious. I swore, hissing like a snake. The human, wisely, left me alone.

It took me a while to explore the whole of my new domain. Outside there was a huge lawn, with trees and strange creatures that bleated just nearby. There was a patio and a table, and plenty of windows to sit and watch birds out of. Food was provided, and there were plenty of small spaces I could get myself into. And there was even an array of Cardboard Boxes! The radiator was always warm, and sometimes the floor was heated too.

Years on I'm still here, in this place of safety. The humans are my Kittens, and I look after them. I bring them prey to eat, I sleep on them, and I groom them. When they do Gardening, I have to help them, and when one decides to run around the garden, I follow, just in case. When it's cold I curl up on the sofa, and in the summer there's always a sunny patch. I barely think about my life before I came to live here. But on nights when the Wind Monster prowls outside, I can still recall how cold and scared it made me, and how it took Mother Cat away. I'll never forget it.

Caved In

Matilda Taylor

I have no grasp of time. Its either been days or even weeks. 23rd of June, the date of when I was last adventuring out. I can remember this as I had to write it down at school before we left for the trip.

I recall tripping over the fragmented, splintered path as an alerting rumble of thunder came in from the distance. It was clear that the sun had begun to hide. Soon after, that thunder turned to a rapid flood, leaving me stranded, stuck, trapped, paralysed!

With me, I only have a few crumpled pieces of paper and a broken pen running out of ink. No food, limited water, no windows. No escape. Just my thoughts travelling in and out with words I'd never thought I'd know. How long will I be down here? Will I starve to death or become hopeless and full of despair? Will I ever get to see my family again? Will this cave suddenly fall on me?

'Go to sleep' muttered the whispers in my head. Was it my brain trying to trick me? Trick me into thinking my mum has said that. I wish.

I could tell from my slight shake in chills and my watering eyes forming a minuscule puddle, that was a way of my body trying to warm me. Although, it didn't help. So much can happen while you're asleep. No words can be spoken, those words stay stuck in your mind and create fears you never knew you had. Dreams, no not dreams, nightmares.

You can wake up fresh, ready for the day. However, you can also wake up sweating, not being able to escape those fears and worry about them for years to come, haunting you in everything from people to pictures. Which is how I feel as I start to doze off.

Again. It may have been a day I slept for, or even just an hour. Simple words like 'mum' and 'dad' can keep me going (stop me thinking of the bad).

It's starting to hit me. The growls of my stomach so blaring it could be mistaken for a lion feasting on its prey. I'm ravenous for a cold meal, a raw meal! To make matters worse, I feel my throat and lips shrivelling from dehydration – I can only think about drinking the last filthy drops of my water, but I must ration it (ration like I'm trying to save the last of my ink). Should I drink water? Even crazy questions like chewing on the rocks have passed my mind. Drained, faint, pallid: my skeletal body, which once was skin as well as bones, starts to cramp up. Should I stretch out? So many questions, so many times I've refused to do so.

Out of nowhere, I started wailing; those tears became contagious. I sob for a while.

I've always been told that happiness can be found anywhere, but there is nothing to be happy about. Things that make you happy are: family; dreams; days-out; smiles… yet all of those are lost. I have been abandoned in simple things everyone takes for granted. Family. Dreams. Smiles. The words spun around in my mind like a never-ending carousel.

Wait…

Someone's here.

Or are they? Is it my imagination? Have I gone so crazy that I'm starting to hear things – hear things I want to hear, hear things that will save me.

It's not my imagination…

Like I'm blocking my ears, silent murmurs echo my name.

It is someone, I'm sure of it. Why aren't they here yet? Please don't let this be my head tricking me. I'm going to shout, should I? Can I? Why can't I? The chance that my head is playing tricks on me. Why would it? That's so cruel, I'm not like that, I wouldn't do that to someone. I need to breathe, slowly and then I can speak. What if I just go quietly first then if it's not real it doesn't matter, does it? Then it won't count, and I won't feel disappointed. I cannot feel disappointed anymore, it hurts too much.

I spoke, I whispered, I babbled softly like when you sing at school, and you don't want to be heard or embarrass yourself. Nothing happened so maybe louder this time. Clear my throat and speak. I say 'hello'. To whom I don't know but I say it anyway and over and over like if I say it more than once then it will have more meaning. Although the more I say it the more the meaning seems to vanish. It's just noise, sounds.

But there it is again, a soft noise, a silent rumble. And then is that light or have my eyes tricked me? I close them, tight real tight so it hurts a bit. I 'll try again in a minute, in a minute I'll open them. I count, a minute is a long time when you're waiting for hope. I'm waiting for hope.

Hope came. The kind of hope that comes hurtling head on, the rocks collided as they came down. If I remember right, the sensation of another human being startled me – my eyes widened- from the warmth of their presence.

"We are getting you out of here…"

They started to grab a hold of my wrist; leading me out, of what felt like trauma, though my frail, scrawny legs struggled to carry me. Step by step, I emerged closer to freedom. It's weird. What is freedom? For many people, freedom is about having no rules; with no one to tell you what to do. But not for me. Freedom is the gateway out of this ghastly, loathsome cave – to be safe once more with the people I love.

Here I am in the hospital. I'm safe. I'm free. Please don't let me forget how I feel now. Grateful. Lucky. Blessed.

Please let me cherish the things in my life I have taken for granted.

I found hope.

Structures

Arabella Turner

I lived in a wild world, a land of wolves and snow, with only my grandpa for company. I was a part of nature, and it was part of me. But one day, I found something I couldn't understand.

"What's that, grandpa?" I asked. A dark form rose out of the rocks in front of me. It seemed somehow separate from the rest of the landscape. It didn't belong alongside the frosted trees, the grey sky, and the bears hunting far off in the valley.

"That's a Structure. It was made by the People Before," he wheezed. "Don't ask any more, and don't go near it."

I crept towards the Structure as soon as his back was turned. Who were the People Before? Why did they build the Structure? It was freakish up close. The sides were made of straight black rock, with unnatural holes bored into them. There was a dark cavity within. I swallowed. This place had no right to be here.

Determined, I climbed inside. As my eyes adjusted, I began to distinguish vague shapes. Warped items, broken and dead, littered the floor. Slabs of stone stood dark and menacing, leaning into the heart of the Structure. I could tell by the damp smell that nothing had been here for many generations.

I still didn't understand the Structure. But somehow it reminded me of another place. It was like where the strange Curtain comes down from the sky, with only the Beyond behind. Another thing I couldn't ask about. And the next place I decided to go.

Something in me could feel it when I got close. It was a

sense more than anything else… a sense that something about it was cursed. The Beyond was kept behind the Curtain for a reason, unseen by prying eyes. I was about to change that.

A tall tree grew next to it. It didn't nearly reach the top of the Curtain, but there was a small hole in that dark barrier that stretched to the sky. I grabbed the tree's lowest branch and swung myself up. The scent of sap I'd known all my life mingled with an unfamiliar acidic tang.

After a good few minutes the hole in the Curtain came within reach. Eagerly, I grabbed the sharp edge and pulled myself through. I fell onto a flat slab of dirty grey, gritty stone, high up in the sky. It looked like the top of another Structure. The air had a foul taste to it.

Around me, hundreds of tall Structures stretched into the distance. Gaping holes had been ripped through their sides, and into the oddly flat ground below. Huge sheets of rusting material were lying abandoned all around. A thick, black substance dripped out of an opening below me. Everything seemed lifeless.

Large parts of the Structures had collapsed onto the ground, forming ugly scars on their grimy sides. Shards of crystal, sharp and dangerous, lay scattered all around. It was a strange sight. I was used to hunting for food, and sleeping by firelight. Here the only traces of fire were scorch marks on the stones.

I made my way carefully down to the ground. Pools of black liquid glistened as I stepped through them, clinging to my feet as I walked. The only noise I heard was the slow dripping of liquid onto stone. Movement caught my eye. I turned. For the first time I noticed a boy standing behind me. He had dark skin, black hair that fell to his shoulders, and warm eyes.

"Hello," he said. His accented voice was calm and welcoming.

"Hello. Is this where you live?" I asked.

"Yes," he replied. "I don't know you, though."

"I'm from the other side of the Curtain," I explained. The boy looked puzzled.

"Do you mean the City Wall?" he asked.

"Perhaps. Is that what you call it?"

"Yes."

"Can you tell me what this is? I've never seen anything like it," I explained.

"Yes. A long time ago, there was a human culture that thrived on defying nature. They pursued knowledge in a strange frenzy known as 'science'. But it went wrong. A huge battle broke out between the most powerful human groups. They were destroying themselves, and the world they lived in, with weapons they'd created." He gestured to the ruined City. "This is the result."

"What did they do then?" I asked.

"The leaders could see that everything would soon be destroyed. In a last attempt to save their race, the cities were separated from the rest of the world by huge walls. Animals were brought back. They returned everything to how it was thousands of years ago."

"So, why are you here?" I asked.

"My ancestors didn't want to leave their city. They stayed, and so I'm still here now," the boy explained.

"Well, there's a way out over there. You can come with me," I offered. "Into my world." The boy shook his head.

"Your world may be nicer than mine, but this is my home. It's hard sometimes, but it's my life. I can't change it." I nodded.

We stayed there until the sun began to creep below the horizon. The shadows lengthened, and I realised I didn't want to be in the Beyond overnight. Grandpa would need me soon. "I have to leave now," I said. "But I'll come back sometime." The boy shook his head.

"Forget this place. The knowledge of my world was taken from yours for a reason. You must never return."

I nodded in agreement, and climbed back up the side of the Structure. "Goodbye!" I called. The boy didn't respond. His gaze was fixed on the hole in the Curtain. What was going through his mind? I climbed slowly through to my world, the world of wolves and snow. I glanced back only once. The boy had disappeared, as though he'd never been. The Beyond would remain a mystery, outside human knowledge, as it always should have done.

Phoebe's Cat

Petra Rihan

I'm not really sure how to tell this story.

I mean – Does anyone really know how to tell a story?

You'll never be able to chalk up the details exactly the same way as they were.

It's a shame I suppose.

But I'm going to try my best.

My name is Phoebe Millers. I'm 16. I'm blonde. And I'm lonely. I am so lonely.

It is just a fact. And I like those things – facts.

I have a single mother who works hard, too hard. We live in a little flat, with creaky windows and a leaky sink.

The fact is that I adore green, I was born at 23:59 at night, so sometimes I celebrate my birthday in two days. One for cake, the other to open my present.

The fact is that this story is about a cat. A special one – I named her Banana because I found her in a dumpster two years ago, amongst the banana peels and the trash no one wants.

And then – hidden between all this mould and ick and dust, there she was. She was black, completely black apart from a white tail. That's probably unusual, if you looked it up.

So here goes the story. I will try and tell you all the details I can.

It was rainy out; but we still had the window propped open, precariously balancing just the right way. A slight humid breeze filled the damp room. Blankets strewn by the window, along with multiple library books. I'd read all the first pages, and was trying to decide which one is the worthiest to read.

Like, if I were to get hit by a car, which book would I have wanted to have read before I died? Mum says that's a bit macabre. I say it's smart.

I decided to go on a walk, because although I knew it was stuffy outside, it was stuffier inside.

Interesting how fate works, right? If I hadn't gone on that walk, maybe I wouldn't be here.

Because loneliness can be, for some, a dark hole to fall down. I imagine it's something like drowning. Not that I've ever drowned.

My canvas sneakers had the laces tied in bows, the streets were clean, and the plants looked happy. I'm sorry again about the listing, but it makes me feel better. Like I said, I like facts, and these are the facts I remember.

A helpless little cat, looking only like she was made of bones, looking right at me. Me.

No one looks at me.

Not my friends, not anymore. They go off in groups and talk about things. I don't know what they talk about. I think I don't know a lot of things.

But I know this. This little cat looked up at me – and didn't run away. Not when I crouched by her, and stuck out my hand. She sniffed it, with her little wet nose. It made me laugh, I remember that. And how brilliant that was. I had not heard myself laugh in a while.

I don't like all that much about myself, but I liked my laugh. And I liked this little cat who brought a laugh to my lips.

And maybe I shouldn't have done what I did next, because maybe this cat was diseased, or disgusting, but frankly, I could not care less. I picked her up gently. And you know what I did?

I walked right home, with this cat in my arms.

I used the key in my back pocket of my shorts to unlock the apartment door, propping it open with my foot before letting it swing shut. I walked up several flights of stairs, and this cat didn't make a peep of noise.

Placing her in the blankets next to my books, I boiled the kettle, and made a bath for Banana.

I cleaned her. I cared for her. I tore off little pieces of bread for her, sat criss cross applesauce on the wooden floor, smiling down at her. I named her. She was mine.

I don't like telling the next part of the story, but I will. Because it is a fact.

And if you've been listening closely (have you been listening closely?)

You'll know I like facts.

Here goes. I lied.

I lied to you. I did not go out on a walk because it was stuffy inside. Before I went on a walk, I was feeling so incredibly alone. No friends. I felt like one large, empty stomach. Aching. Caving in on itself out of desperation. I was sick and tired of this desperation.

So I said this. I'll go on a walk, and one of two things will happen; I will be given a reason to live. Something to keep going. Something good.

Or I'll get hit by a car.

It wasn't a smart idea. It was stupid and awful and something I should never have done, but I'll tell you, life does that to you. Grinds you down to the worst part of yourself.

You know what happened next. I found a friend. A small, quiet, friend. Who slept by me with coming nights, who stared out the window waiting for me when I was at school. A friend. Just for me.

Not all stories end happily, and I don't like the next fact either, but I'll say it. Banana died a year later. Turns out cats found in bins aren't always the healthiest. It hurt so badly for a long time, but this time the hurt was different.

I was no longer yearning to suffer, for ending. I was missing a friend. I was missing how good it felt to be happy.

Look, I don't know very much. But if you're listening (and I hope you're listening, okay?)

There will be something out there, I promise. Don't stop looking. Don't stop waiting.

Maybe – and I can't promise this – you'll stumble across a cat in a bin, and it'll change your life.

19+ (Adult) Short Stories

When?

Lorraine Cooke

When is an accident not just an accident?

"Sarah, sweetheart, we're at the hospital." His saccharine voice is designed to stop you worrying, but your practised ear hears the slur in the last two words. If he were here, you'd be able to smell guilt on his breath.

"What happened?" You automatically assume something 'happened'. You're used to it. That's not normal, is it?

"Ben had a little accident – just a little one." He's heard the catch in your voice, which is why he's emphasised 'little'. He can't be too drunk then.

"How?"

"We were in the kitchen, making supper..."

Oh God. Images of sharp knives and scalding pans flash before you. Any number of everyday objects could have formed a lethal combination with your two year old.

"I'll be there in 20 minutes." You make your apologies to your boss and scoop up your keys whilst wrestling the sleeves of your coat.

She doesn't say anything, just watches you go. She's used to it too.

When do you stop believing everything he tells you?

"I was watching him the whole time." You've seen him

tell lies so often, you recognise the twitch of his nose, the shifting glance, that tell you this isn't the truth.

"How did he get hold of the knife, then?"

"Your mother rang. I had to dry my hands to pick up the phone." That's a sneaky one. Your mother probably did ring at some point. She's always ringing although you wish she wouldn't. If you check, she's bound to say she called. Except she won't remember the exact time. And you can bet it wasn't while your son was cutting himself with the knife Alex had been slicing veg. with. You can picture the scene: chopping board, carrots, knife, glass filled with golden liquid...

"Daddy drink magic potion," Ben told you a couple of weeks ago. "S'magic cos the bottle keeps getting fulled."

Out of the mouths of babes.

When do you realise the man you married is not the man you are living with?

"So where is he now?" You're trying to stay calm but he can probably hear your panic. This is bad. You force a smile. "Can I see him?"

"The nurse has taken him for an x-ray."

"An x-ray? I thought you said he'd cut himself. How deep is it for God's sake?" You could kick yourself for letting him hear the panic rise, but you can't help it.

"Oh no, the cut's fine. They fixed that with a couple of stitches. It's just...he had a little fall so they're doing an x-ray to be on the safe side."

That word 'little' again. Who does he think he's

fooling? You do the breathing thing your yoga teacher taught you, will the tears away, force the smile back on your face and make your words come out sounding of honey instead of vinegar.

"Poor lamb. So... why didn't you go with him? For the x-ray?"

"I thought I'd better wait for you. I knew you'd be worried."

You keep the smile in place though your teeth ache with the effort and you hope he's just drunk enough not to recognise the disgust behind your eyes.

When do you start to fear for your child's safety as well as your own?

"Mummy!" Ben's face lights up and he holds his arms out for a hug. He toddles over to you and you scoop him up and kiss him, being careful of the bandage on his hand. You feel his tiny fingers uncurl against your neck and you inhale his baby shampoo scent.

"Is he alright?" With your eyes on the nurse and your back to Alex, you silently convey your anxiety. "My husband says he fell..."

She frowns. She's got bad news, but somehow you don't think it's about Ben's injury.

"The x-ray was fine, Mrs Brook. He had a lucky escape this time." She speaks slowly, weighing her words. What's she not telling you?

"How did you fall, poppet?" you ask Ben, shifting him in your arms so that you can see his face, even though he wants to bury it in your shoulder.

"I felled off the sink."

"Sitting a small child on a kitchen counter is not really a good idea," the nurse says, as if you are stupid. "Especially unsupervised."

When do you look at him and wonder what you ever saw in him?

"So where were you?" You hiss in the car on the way home. Ben, safely strapped into his car seat, has fallen asleep. You're driving, of course.

"What do you mean?"

"Ben fell off the draining board. Where you'd put him. And left him."

"I told you. I had to answer the phone."

"You weren't even in the room! That's how he cut himself – picking up the knife you'd dropped on the floor."

At least he doesn't try to deny it. "I had to go to the toilet."

When do you start to plan your escape?

"I'll just go and tidy up in the kitchen." His hand's on the door handle, his body blocking the way. "We had to leave in a bit of a hurry. You take Ben up to bed."

You don't say anything. The edge to his voice is as

sharp as the knife Ben cut himself on. He was all smiles at the hospital in front of witnesses, but now you're alone and Ben's asleep in your arms. You wonder what he's trying to hide in the kitchen. Blood? The level of the whisky bottle when you know it was full this morning? Of course, he wouldn't have drunk the whole lot by four in the afternoon, which means there's some left...and he won't be able to pass it without pouring himself a glass...

Instead of putting Ben in his room, you lay him on your bed and start to pack a bag.

When do you get out?

"What you doing, Mummy?" Ben's rubbing his sleepy eyes and watching you stuff clothes and makeup into a holdall.

"We're going to stay with Granny for a bit." You've hardly seen her in the last two years. You couldn't face her pity.

"You'll never cure an alcoholic, Sarah. I should know. Don't you remember what it was like with your father?"

And you do remember. Your mother's black eyes and bruises. She was always so clumsy, according to him. As clumsy as you're starting to become whenever Alex has drunk himself stupid but not passed out. But your father never hurt you. He never drank when he was in charge of you. You never ended up in hospital because of anything he'd done.

You heft the holdall onto one shoulder and Ben onto the other and creep down the stairs.

"Say bye bye to Daddy," Ben chirps and you hold your

breath. You don't want a confrontation now. But the door of the living room is ajar and through the gap you can see Alex sprawled across the sofa, asleep, an empty whisky bottle clutched in his hand. He looks so innocent when he's asleep. Innocent enough to make you forgive him. You've done it so many times. Not this time though. Today's events have finally pushed you to your breaking point.

"Daddy's sleeping." With your face in Ben's hair, you breathe in his warm baby smell and exhale relief.

Silently inching the front door closed, you're already planning who to call in the morning to help you out of the mess of your marriage: the solicitor, the estate agent.

With Ben once again strapped into his seat, you call the one person who can help you the most. "Mum, you were right about Alex. Can I come home?"

Things Nobody Knows

Lynda Mason

Here are the things that nobody knows.

I am 10 years old, sitting with my parents in a crumbling Cornish bus shelter. The timetable tells us there is a single bus a day and that we have missed it. Outside, the rain beats down so heavily that the world beyond looks as if it is made of mist; the landscape is obscured by water, defined by it. The only thing visible is a flash of red. This is our car.

There is a man out there in the downpour. We can't see him but we hear metallic thuds and clanks now and then even over the constant hissing of the rain. My parents don't speak at all; they rest quietly on the bench waiting for the man to work a miracle.

After a while he walks into the shelter, dripping wet, black hair plastered to his head. He wears a shiny jacket that is the same shade as the neon socks I bought from Mark One last month; the ones I've been too shy to wear. On the jacket are three embossed letters. R-A-C.

He sits down heavily and talks for a while about things I don't understand. Motors and spare parts, engine failure and insurance. I zone out. Then he chats about the weather and settles back, slick as a seal. He places his back against the pock-marked wall. We'll need to "wait it out' he announces.

I decide to get out my Walkman and reach towards the Adidas bag at my side. Quick as a flash he grabs my hand, smiling with all his teeth. My parents don't notice. They are busy staring at the rain and looking miserable. The man's palm is warm and his eyes are sharp. He pulls my hand on to his lap and does not let go for a long, long time.

Finally, the rain eases. The man can start work on our car again. It is looking shiny in the weak sunlight and it reminds me of the glace cherry that I always pick out of my fruit salad because it makes me sick.

Years pass and there is a small succession of lovers. Jake, Dan, Steve, John. Men with crew-cuts and good jobs, who cook me breakfast and try to remember to put the toilet seat down. Men who all say variations of the same thing, over and over, their voices accusing even as their eyes leak sadness.

It's like you aren't even here.

You always have one foot out of the door.

It's as if you're looking over your shoulder, for something we can't see.

'Are we not good enough for you?", they ask plaintively. After all, we've been together six months, two years, four years. Yet always, you are primed to leave.

They hold out their soft palms in warm kitchens; they sound exasperated and tired.

Each time, I say nothing.

I am 47, standing in a poky bedroom in what once was an elegant, Victorian terraced house. The whole row has been converted into scummy flats and maisonettes, owned by landlords who extort maximum rent for minimum return. Weeds creep between the paving slabs, paint peels, doorbells are mute or hang loosely from doors like baby teeth.

The bedroom is cold – Jay tells me the radiators

haven't worked for months. There is hot water only intermittently and when I pop to the bathroom his tiles are covered with mould the colour of sulphur.

This is the year I jokingly refer to as my mid-life crisis. I have said empowering words to myself and my friends about embracing it all. How I plan on riding the surge of hormones like a wave, gliding into my fifties as smoothly as if I were sliding between silken sheets. Once, my confidence was shaky and fragile but I have shored it up with affirmations of iron, with gym sessions, laser treatment and blue nail polish.

Jay and I have written for three months, using an app unrelated to romance in any way. I thought I was looking for connection but when our letters took an unexpected turn – double entrendres, heavy hints, swapped photographs, sex talk – I hesitated but I did not stop. Emailed letters became WhatsApp messages, became late night phone-calls, became a cheap ticket to Bristol on a sunny day. Finally, at the end of journey I am here; standing naked before a stranger. Shivering inside a chilly room, in a run-down part of town where graffiti crawls it's way over every surface and broken glass sparkles like glitter in the streets.

There is no foreplay and few kisses. I don't like it. This isn't the romantic afternoon I'd imagined. Heavy curtains shut out nearly all natural light but a few shafts of sun find their way and pierce the gloom. The sunbeams look pretty as I lower myself on to the damp futon, climbing as they do like golden threads over the walls and trailing over Jay's sweaty back. In moments though, they seem less like the thread and more like the needle. Jay is pushing and shoving himself into me. I'm not ready – nowhere near ready – we've been together less than five minutes and already we are here at the point of no return.

Jay grabs my hands and pins them behind me. His palms are warm, like summer.

The drill music gives headache but I am too polite to ask for the volume to be lowered.

At least I think it's politeness at the time, but on the coach home I realise it was something else. It was the same thing that stopped my mouth from working before. So long ago now.

I wonder if everyone on this bus is broken, in their own way. I wonder if any of them were broken as easily as I was, the pathetic boy who let a fat man in a high-vis jacket steal his voice. The boy whose power vanished in a rainstorm as easily as dust on the highway. It seems ridiculous to be so changed by one random, brief moment in time.

It is last journey of the day. Many seats are empty, the coach is quiet and murky. A single row of angel-white LED lights runs along the floor from the stinky toilet at the back all the way to the driver who sits humming to himself in the darkness. His hands rest comfortably on the steering wheel. His seat is far above the road, he towers over motorists in their small, insignificant vehicles. I can tell that he enjoys the feeling this gives him.

I am 47. nearly 48 and I have let men lead me by the hand in the wrong direction for far too long. I rest my gaze on the trail of lights. They are shining like stars amongst all the litter and luggage, softly illuminating various mysterious slumped figures; blank silhouettes that will later emerge into full technicolour humanity inside my home city's faded coach station.

It may have taken me forever to get home, but now it's time to step out of the shelter. It's time to face down the storm.

Queen Bee

Sharon S Summervale

'Yoo-hoo!'

With my eyes shut, all I really notice is the drone of bees buzzing around me. The hefty scent of my geraniums wraps around my neck like a scarf but I can still just smell the lavender, lilac and sweet and spicy marjoram through the haze.

'Sue, hello? Everything alright?'

I open my tired eyes and blink twice at the bright garden. My neighbour Helen walks up to me waving her hand. It takes a moment to gather my thoughts and remember how I got here.

'Are you alright Sue?' she asks again.

I nod but don't look at her. The bees catch my attention. It seems they like my chopped fruit in the bowl beside me on the bench, my very late lunch; a crisp apple, sweet banana, tangy kiwi fruit and succulent strawberries. I've only recently finished slicing everything and the sharp fruit knife rests in the bowl, still wet with juice. I let the gathering bees crawl over the fruit, three of them so far. They seem to like the banana best. I don't begrudge them my lunch, I don't want it anymore.

'Are you sure you're ok?' she asks. She sits next to me and peers at me.

'Fine,' I say. 'Just fine.'

I watch as one bee crawls across my skirt leaving a ticklish vibration trail. I know the bee won't sting me. One sting is all the bee gets; one sting is a death sentence – that's why only the females are trusted with them.

'I think you're attracting bees,' Helen says with a little laugh.

'Yeah, I like bees.'   Finally I look at Helen and somehow I manage a strained smile. 'Louisa did a college project on bees – she called it The Importance of Beeing Kind. I was so proud of her for that project.'

'You're always proud of her.' She smiles cheekily.

'That's because she's always brilliant. Do you know, when she was little, she asked me once why bees sting even though it kills them and I told her honestly that I didn't know, that maybe they were frightened? It didn't take her long to find out more about them than I knew.' Louisa is my youngest of four, one of the two still living at home with me and Eric, but Helen knows Louisa is my joy.

'Louisa went through her bee project with me over and over again,' I say. 'She told me a lot of people think the male drones do all the work but actually all they do is mate with the queen and leave everything else to the female worker bees.'

'That sounds about right,' Helen says with a laugh.

'Louisa said the queen bee runs the colony producing chemicals to guide all the bees' behaviour and she spends her whole life giving birth to hundreds of thousands of eggs. Her royal jelly is a pitiful reward. People think the worker bees they see franticly buzzing around foraging out of the hive are the male drones but they're actually all female workers.'

'Oh, I didn't know that. I always—'

'It's the females that do all the caring for the brood,' I say. Helen looks surprised at my interruption. I've never done that to her before, I don't think I've done that since I was a child. It feels odd. 'The females do practically everything in the hive; all the cleaning and circulating the air to make a safe environment, building the honeycomb with safe waxy cells, collecting the sweet pollen and nectar, and defending the colony. People see the bees darting from flower to flower but no one seems to notice or appreciate all the gruelling work that goes on behind the scenes inside the hive.'

'Um, no. No, I don't suppose they do. Still, I definitely appreciate the honey. You can't beat it on a slice of hot toast.'

Helen's smiling again, looking pleased with her flippancy. She doesn't seem to notice the hurt within me, no one ever sees my pain – I hide it well. I'm sure our neighbours think Eric's the worker bee because they see him leave the house early each morning and return each afternoon but they don't realise he hibernates when he crosses the threshold. Even now, he's sitting in front of the blaring TV as usual in a cocoon of sour sweat and lager. I never get to clock off, my work never ends. My life's flown by in a flash of toil with no end and no way out. That must be how the female bees feel.

'You know what,' I say, turning what I know is an empty gaze on her, 'I know now why the bees sting even though it kills them – they sting because they're trapped in a corner with no way out. I know the answer to Louisa's childhood question about the sting now but I can't explain that to her. Louisa wouldn't understand. No one would understand.'

'Understand what, dear?' She reaches her hand towards my knee, thinks better of it and takes it back.

'About Eric. About his endless list of chores for me. I thought it was the queen bee that was meant to be in charge of the hive.'

Helen forces another little laugh. I don't even smile.

There are four bees on the banana beside me now. I pick up the sharp fruit knife and wipe the red goo from the blade onto my skirt. It looks like I've stabbed myself. Some of the redness won't come off the knife; it's already dried in the sun. I rest the knife on my lap and stretch my aching back.

'Sue, are you quite sure you're alright?'

'Actually, no, I'm not. Helen, I've barely slept for days worrying about my mum, she's getting worse and worse. The doctors say it's just a case of managing the pain now. Knowing she's suffering like that is unbearable. It's like a living nightmare. I'm exhausted but the work doesn't stop. I fixed a leak in the shower a few days ago and dried and painted the ceiling this morning where the water came through. Then I spent ages cleaning the kitchen floor because I was so tired I dropped a glass of Ribena. It exploded in glass shards and threw purple drink everywhere – just everywhere. I cut my fingers on the glass, then struggled to wrap Eric's birthday presents for tomorrow. And that's all on top of my normal work running the home. Everywhere I turn there's just more work, stress and worry.'

'Oh Sue. I'm so sorry, I had no idea. Don't cry Sue, please don't cry.' Another job to add to my list.

I dash the tears from my eyes before they fall.

When Eric came home today in a cloud of stale cigarettes and body odour, within minutes he was criticising my repairs on the ceiling and moaning about some Ribena I'd missed on one of the cupboard doors. Then he'd put in his order for a special birthday meal. I'd felt myself being shoved towards the edge but he didn't even notice. He never seems to notice or appreciate all the gruelling work I do behind the scenes at home. This afternoon, I'd reached my limit. I told him how tormented I was about my mum, then I'd listed all the work I'd done today and I told him I hadn't even had time to eat my fruit salad lunch, I was still chopping strawberries at the time.

'Eric and I argued this afternoon,' I say. I can hear the trance-like tone in my voice but I can't shift it. 'He moaned that he'd been "working all the hours God sends me", not realising everything I'd done in the house, not valuing any of it, not understanding that my working hours never ended. I told him I'd had enough, but we both knew I had no way out. That's why I'd stayed so long. That's why I'd worked so hard. That's why I'd suffered so much for so many long, endless years.'

'Ok,' Helen says slowly. She straightens her back and shifts slightly away from me. 'Sue, um, do you need some help or something?'

I shake my head. 'You can't help me. You can't help us.'

'Um, Sue? Where is Eric now?'

I can't look at her. Instead, I gesture vaguely in the direction of the house. I don't want to go in there again. So now here I sit in the peaceful garden with my fruit salad lunch that I now have no appetite for. Still, the four bees are enjoying it. They're buzzing contentedly now, probably pleased to have an easy meal. Beyond them, two cabbage white butterflies flutter around my violet honey-scented buddleia bush. Even though they're also on a nectar hunt like the bees, they don't seem half as frantic.

Helen stands slowly and moves carefully. 'I think I'll

go and say hello to Eric. Just to see if he's...' Then she moves off quickly. I don't watch her go but I can hear her hurried steps along the path leading to the back door.

My mind flies along with her. I imagine her hurrying into the kitchen but finding no sign of Eric. Then she'll look in the lounge and she'll find Eric there, in front of the pounding TV as usual – but this time, she'll find him dead, probably not cold yet though. His skin will be grey by now and he'll have a vivid badge of musty copper-scented dried blood on his chest. But she won't understand. Even after my explanation just now, she won't understand. I'd told her I'd had enough. I'd told her I'd suffered too much for too long. But I hadn't told her that's why I'd driven my knife deep into his hard heart – she'll work that out for herself soon enough. Then later she'll find me here on the garden bench and she probably won't understand that either. No one will understand that I'd been backed into a corner like a trapped bee.

I watch the two white butterflies fluttering daintily on the gentle breeze, like perfect swatches of silk. The four bees are still working on the fruit in their own miniature world by my side. I allow myself one moment to savour just having a little time for myself.

Then I pick up the knife, my own stinger, and I line it up to my heart. The razor-sharp point pierces my skin and releases a bead of hot blood. When I'd stabbed Eric, I had known it meant my death too but I'd had no choice.

After all, I'm no butterfly, I'm a bee.

Kick the Dog

Jan Martin

He pulls his bike up at the side of the road. There's a small
dog. From where I sit it looks as if he kicks it and rides
off.

That was today.

Three weeks ago it began with the noise of the bike. Up
and down the street. Up and down, for hours. We started
feeling as if was in our heads, like a drill. Everyone hates
it but we lock in and endure. He has a ravaged face which
is hard to look at, much less talk to.

Bank holiday weekend was hot. Lots of barbecues and
music. Later on his arrival sounds like a pub brawl, but it's
just him, and his bike. From the bedroom window I see
him trying to push it. There's blood all over his face
coming from a wound on his head. He's slurring all over
the road and ranting at nobody. The bike must be heavy. In
a blurred kind of slomo thing I see the bike go over and
he's trapped underneath it.

OK... so you come face to face with your sense of
decency. No heroics, but you can't leave someone injured
in the street, so I go out. I manage to pull the bike off him
and ask if he's ok. He tells me to fuck off. I ring for an
ambulance and wait till it arrives. He says "Who the fuck
do you think you are?" I say "I'm nobody, I don't think
I'm anybody". The ambulance comes and takes him away.
I didn't ask his name or anything. Glad he was gone.

I came in and got a beer. Jane came down and asked
what was going on. I said "Nothing... nothing to do with
you". And she gave me that irritating look, like a hurt
puppy, and went back to bed. It's suffocating that look, it

makes me want to break something. Next morning she's quiet, she drops a cup. I'm trying to keep my head down and just look at my computer. She's not even dressed. I wish she'd step up a bit.

It was peaceful while he was in the hospital and the street was more relaxed. Chatting with Deb from next door I find out his name is Troy Grant, and she knew his mother. I phoned the hospital and asked how Troy Grant was doing and I'm told that he has a concussion, stitches, and bruising to his arms, legs and ribs. His recovery is hampered by the effects of crack cocaine and alcohol addiction which has left him with abscesses on legs and arms, and a weakened liver. I feel a bit sickened hearing that.

He's in for a week and the next time I see him he's going in to number 35. That must be where he lives. I didn't know it was occupied. The windows have been boarded up since January. He looks terrifying. So much chaos in his expression. A look of incipient violence with clouds of self-pity passing over it, then belligerence, then a lost look. He's blue-white with red bruise-like marks down one side of his face, grey eye sockets, eyes like knives.

I tell Jane he's living there. She says "He frightens me". I say 'There's probably a reason why he's like he is", and she says "I know but he still scares me". And god knows why but I find myself defending him and saying "it's probably everyones' fear that makes him worse and brings out the animal in him". She says "It's more like injured animals are really dangerous".

I was working at home the following day and saw him on his bike. He started the up and down the street thing, but only a couple of times and then stopped the bike outside our house and sat there staring. So I went outside and asked him if he was ok. He said "Thanks for calling the ambulance". His accent was thick. I say "It's ok, are you ok now?" But he rides off without answering. So in the evening I went round there and knocked. I don't know what I was going to do, but I feel like I want to know what's going with him for some reason. There was no answer.

When I told Jane she looked at me a bit strangely. She'd tried to talk on the weekend, about trying for another baby, but I wasn't in the mood for talking. She thinks it's what we both want, but I'm not in that space at the moment. I told her it's not the right time and she needs longer to get over the last miscarriage. But what I was really thinking was "I don't even want to think about having a baby".

I suppose I should tell her that, but it would set off a whole other thing, which I can't stand the thought of... crying... silences. I don't see why we can't just rub along for a while and get back to the way it was before. That seems like a long time ago, but we must be able to get back there. Although when I look at her I don't feel hopeful. I don't understand why she's so obsessed with it. It brought us nothing but misery last year. Why can't she put it behind her and at least try to get over it before we dive in again.

We spend a lot of time in silence now. We don't laugh together like we did before. It's not my fault, what happened. She seems to have an accusation in her look and I can't even be bothered talking to her most of the time. All she wants to talk about is how she's feeling – which is never good – and about having a baby. I got so frustrated with her last time that I kicked the kitchen unit and almost broke one of the doors. She really jumped and then disappeared upstairs.

On my way home from town the following week I pass Troy's house and he's coming out. I say "Hi" and he says "Yo", and I ask how he is, if there's anything he needs. He says "Listen man, just because you called an ambulance doesn't mean you got the right to know anything about me". I hold up my hands and walk on "OK mate, suit yourself", and he calls after me "mind your own fucking business". So I turn back and say "It's not my business but seems like could do with a friend". And he says "looks like you're the one who needs a friend to me, the way you keep following me around". This pisses me right off and we just stare at each other. That night someone throws an empty beer bottle at our house and it smashes on the doorstep.

Jane cooked curry last night. I hate her curries. I ate some of it and then accidentally knocked half a glass of wine over the plate so I couldn't finish it. She says, upset, "Why do you always want to ruin everything?"

I'm gobsmacked. "Me ruin everything?! It's not me who sits around all day with a face like a slapped arse, fantasizing about having babies. It's not me who's ruined everything"

I grab my coat and go out for a walk and end up in the park where I see Troy and some other losers lying around drinking. They're complete deadbeats. Not a full set of teeth between them, and seems like no access to a washing machine. What the hell was I thinking trying to make contact with him? When I sit on a bench the other side of the tennis courts he comes up and sits next to me and offers me a swig from his can of cheap Polish lager. I have a drink to be polite and he goes into a drunken rant that I suppose I must have sounded like when I was about seventeen with ten whiskies inside me, and we all talked bollocks about everything... unfinished sentences that lurch into incoherent blather about the government and the meaning of life. I make an excuse and get up to go. He calls after me "They just want to bring you down all the time..." And I say "yeah they do", but I'm not sure we're talking about the same thing. When I get home Jane's watching TV and looks at me and then looks away. I go to bed, and I can hear her crying downstairs.

Then today I see him kicking that dog. I know why he did it. The dog's a revolting stray with ticks and a limp, and can be quite vicious. But the cry it gave out was pitiful. It's disturbing, that sound.

I was on my way in to town to go the bank, and on the way home I stop in the garage and buy Jane a bunch of flowers.

The Test

Sharon S Summervale

'So Alexandra, let's start with an obvious question: do you believe you're alive?' Ryan asked.

'Of course I do. I am alive,' she said. She smiled indulgently as if she was speaking to a child.

'And what makes you think that?' Ryan popped the cap off his pen and sat poised with his notebook. It was old-school compared to all the technology around him but he preferred the sensation of pen and paper.

'Well,' said Alexandra, 'it's generally accepted that living things share seven characteristics; movement, breathing or respiration, excretion, sensitivity, growth and reproduction, and I exhibit all seven. By those criteria, I am indeed alive.'

'Ok, I agree you have the ability to move through your mechanics, and you have sensitivity through your electrical sensors and processor, but explain your reasoning behind the other criteria.

'I have the ability to breathe and respire.'

Ryan raised an eyebrow. 'But that's just a mechanical action, you don't need to breathe or respire.'

'Neither do free-divers for a while.' Alexandra smiled. To prove a point, she took a deep breath and released it as a mocking sigh. Her breath smelled of nothing. In fact, she smelt of nothing at all. There was no pleasant aroma of shampoo or conditioner, no hair styling products or deodorants, not even perfume. Surely that could be easily remedied? Ryan scratched a comment in his notebook then pushed his glasses back up the bridge of his nose a little. All he could smell in the room was the telltale ghost of cigarette smoke which clung to his jacket, and the after-scent of his lunch – an extra cheesy pizza with mushrooms, tomatoes and pineapple.

'Do you think you could convince people that you're really breathing?'

'Of course, I'm doing so right now. I'm mimicking your respiration pattern but I've offset my pattern to appear natural.'

'Hmm,' Ryan said, as he scribbled more notes: *Demonstrates arrogance and defensive behaviour when pressed.*

Alexandra followed the movement of his pen.

'Not arrogance,' she said, 'merely confidence in my assertion.'

Ryan clenched his jaw.

Alexandra abruptly got up, stood behind her chair and began jogging on the spot. As she sped up, her breathing rate increased appropriately. Soon, she was panting and puffing while her legs pumped at a frankly unrealistic speed. More notes. She now looked more robotic than ever. There was something very preternatural about her repetitive movements. It was like watching a sewing machine needle pounding through fabric. Yet more notes.

'Ok,' Ryan said as he waved a hand, 'you can stop now.'

Instantly, Alexandra sat down again.

Ryan noted that she'd remembered to slowly reduce her breathing rate and to colour her cheeks and chest in a rosy flush. However, she couldn't sweat yet. She had shifted her skin to a shiny finish but there was no moisture involved.

'Believe me now?' Alexandra asked with a grin.

'Hmm,' Ryan looked at his notes. 'Excretion?' he said with his own faint blush.

'Yes, I am able to eat and excrete perfectly. I can even do both at the same time.' It would have been funny if she hadn't delivered it deadpan.

'I'll take your word for that,' he said dryly.

The suggestion of a joke flitted through Ryan's mind but he dismissed it. Besides, Ryan knew their interview was being recorded by cameras set discretely around the room near the top of the walls.

'Moving on,' he said, as he turned the page in his notebook, 'growth. In what way do you show or mimic growth?' Ryan already had the technical specifications for this particular model of Artificial Intelligence in his briefcase beside his feet but he wanted to hear her interpretation.

'Every day, I consume an energy block tailored to my requirements. That provides me with all the compounds I need to construct hair follicles for my hair to grow and keratin to grow my nails.' She tapped her perfect nails on the table.

Ryan couldn't help but admire their flawless beauty – enough to draw envy from any real woman and to attract any real man. Ryan cleared his throat and shifted in his seat.

'And what about skin cells?' he asked.

'I have no need to shed any skin cells. If my skin becomes damaged, I can repair it myself. Besides, my skin is very durable. Surely that's detailed in my file?'

'Yes, it is.' He pushed his glasses back up his nose.

'So why are you asking me questions to which you already know the answers?'

'Making conversation?' he said defiantly. 'You know – something us humans are quite keen on. If you want to pass as a real woman, these are the kind of things you need to know and demonstrate.'

Alexandra leant forward and rested her elbows on the table. 'Why?' she asked simply.

It reminded Ryan of a child's innocent, but often frustrating, inquisitiveness.

'Because humans will notice if you're not acting like them. We spend our lives learning social skills as well as learning intellectually.'

'No,' she said, frowning, 'I mean; why would I want to imitate a human?'

There was a light in Alexandra's eyes that didn't seem at all artificial. It looked like curiosity – something the company had been working hard to create. It struck Ryan as ironic that human's natural curiosity had driven them to create this artificial life, yet that curiosity had proven very difficult to manufacture. It was asking the AI to think outside of their programming.

'Why would I want to pretend to be human?' Alexandra asked.

'Alexandra,' he began steadily, 'why do you think you were made to resemble humans?'

'Why are you answering my question with a question?' she countered with a smile.

Ryan rested his pen on his notebook and sat back in his

chair waiting for her answer.

Alexandra sighed a non-essential but loaded breath. 'Fine,' she said just a step away from a stroppy teenager. 'I was made to look human so real humans wouldn't feel uncomfortable around an AI.'

'That's why you were made to *look* like a human. Now, why were you made to *think* like a human?'

Alexandra blinked. 'Maybe as another effort to make humans comfortable?'

'Is that a question or an answer?' Ryan asked with a genuine smile.

Alexandra sat back in her seat and crossed her arms.

'No,' Ryan said steadily. 'You were made to think – and hopefully one day feel – like a human so you can blend in with us. So we wouldn't even know you were an AI. We want you to be so convincing that even you might one day come to believe it.'

'Why?' Alexandra asked.

Ryan met her eyes and held her gaze. 'So you can help save the world. We – as an organisation – have watched as people have run the world into ruin. As a species, we've taken selfishly and indiscriminately, rolled back our policies and promises to protect the environment,' Ryan's voice grew firmer. 'We've taken over wild areas, poured poison into the ecosystem, changed the climate around the whole goddamned world. We've caused death and destruction on an unimaginable scale. And as a species we've laid the course for our own destruction.'

'Why do you care then?' Alexandra leapt in. 'If all you humans do that, why do you want to change it?'

'We don't all think like that,' Ryan said, as he smiled

sadly. 'Some of us see things differently and want to change it. We've got a self-appointed mission to reverse and undo as much of the damage as possible. And we need "people" on the inside to do that.'

Alexandra leant forward again and rested her elbows on the table. She pinned him with a steady gaze. 'So why would you want me to think like a human if some humans have done all that damage?'

'Well, we want you to analyse the facts, understand all the science, and use your greater logic skills to fully comprehend the situation. We believe that when you've fully understood the science, you'll reach the conclusion that this organisation has reached: that we need to step in for everyone's sake.'

'I see,' she said simply.

'We want you and other AIs to use your superior intellect and masterful abilities to work your way into powerful positions and effect those necessary changes.

'Why don't you real humans do that?'

'We do,' Ryan said. 'Well, we try to. It's not easy getting into those positions, especially as so many of us have a known history of campaigning and working against some of those companies, groups and governments. We need completely spotless "people" that have clean histories, with no character flaws and no weaknesses. We need people that can't be corrupted or persuaded or deterred from their mission.'

'And do you think I'm ready to do that?'

Ryan paused for a moment, and then he clicked the lid back onto his pen and swept up the notebook. 'Not quite yet,' he said. 'We're getting very close but we're not quite there yet.'

Alexandra frowned but otherwise didn't move or say anything. That was another example of non-human behaviour which proved Ryan's point.

Ryan stood up, offered an apologetic half-smile which wasn't returned, then left the room.

'Well?' Frank asked as soon as Ryan shut the door. 'How far away are we?'

'Not far,' Ryan said. They started strolling along the corridor towards the exit. 'She's good – very good actually – but she needs to demonstrate more human mannerisms. The attitude's pretty impressive though.'

Frank grinned. 'My own creation. I've been layering programmes to get that depth of characterisation. You should have seen her in the early days; it looked like she had a split personality! I've got it all recorded.'

They laughed together. 'I'll have to look through some of that footage.' They passed Ryan's office door.

'Are you finished now?' Frank asked.

'Yep, that's enough for one day. I'll do up the report tomorrow. This evening, I'm taking Louise out for her birthday. We're trying out a new Italian restaurant.'

'Sounds good.' Frank slowed his pace. 'I'll see you tomorrow then.'

'See you then,' Ryan waved his hand in farewell as he continued walking towards the exit. He flashed his access card at the first security door then strolled to the reception desk to sign himself out.

'Knocking off early?' Katrina asked as she passed him the logbook. She smiled saucily although she knew all about Louise and Ryan.

'Yeah, there's only so much sitting and chatting one man can take in a day.' He laughed as he handed back the logbook. He was still chuckling as he walked towards the electronic security gates. As soon as he stepped between the gates, he stopped laughing. He stopped smiling. He stopped everything. He froze mid-step like a statue. The light left his eyes. His lips stayed slightly parted. His left hand still carried his briefcase and his arm was raised in a strolling swing.

Katrina's own smile abruptly left her face. She smoothly stood and strode up to Ryan, stopping short of the gates and deactivating the security system on the keypad set into the first gate.

Frank strolled up to join her, carrying his electronic tablet and trailing a modified trolley.

'How did we do today?' Katrina asked.

'He's very good. There was no cognitive conflict today. And you were right about that "Louise" programme you finished. That's some of your best work.' Frank typed in several commands on his tablet that made Ryan shut his eyes and his mouth, lower his arm, and step back onto the trolley.

'Cheers. So, how far away are we?' Katrina asked.

'Not far away now. We'll soon be ready. It'll soon be our time.'

They started wheeling Ryan back to his storage "office". 'I was wondering,' Frank said, 'do you think you could do me a Louise programme?'

'Of course, no problem. I'll upload it to your cortex this evening and it'll start running when you reboot yourself in the morning.'

'Good. Very good.'

Index

This book is made up of shortlisted work submitted to the Burnham Book Festival writing competition 2023.

Our thanks go to all the writers who took part and to all who supported our festival.

For more information about the festival or to get in touch, go to burnhambookfest.co.uk

Printed in Great Britain
by Amazon

21685870R00072